ANIMAL STEW
A Lift-the-Flap Surprise Book

by Shen Roddie · Pictures by Patrick Gallagher

Houghton Mifflin Company

Boston 1991

One day at about lunch time, Eva the Enormous Giant got enormously hungry.

"I could eat an enormous lunch!" she said and flipping through her recipe book, came across one that said:

ANIMAL STEW FOR HUNGRY GIANTS.

Eva the Enormous Giant stalked the countryside looking for things to put into the pot.

She found a caterpillar.
"Good for sweetening the stew!"
she said and dropped Caterpillar
into the sack.

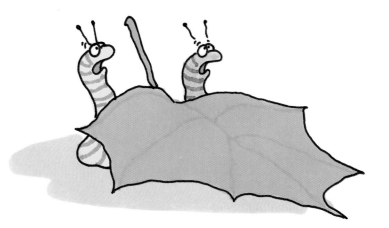

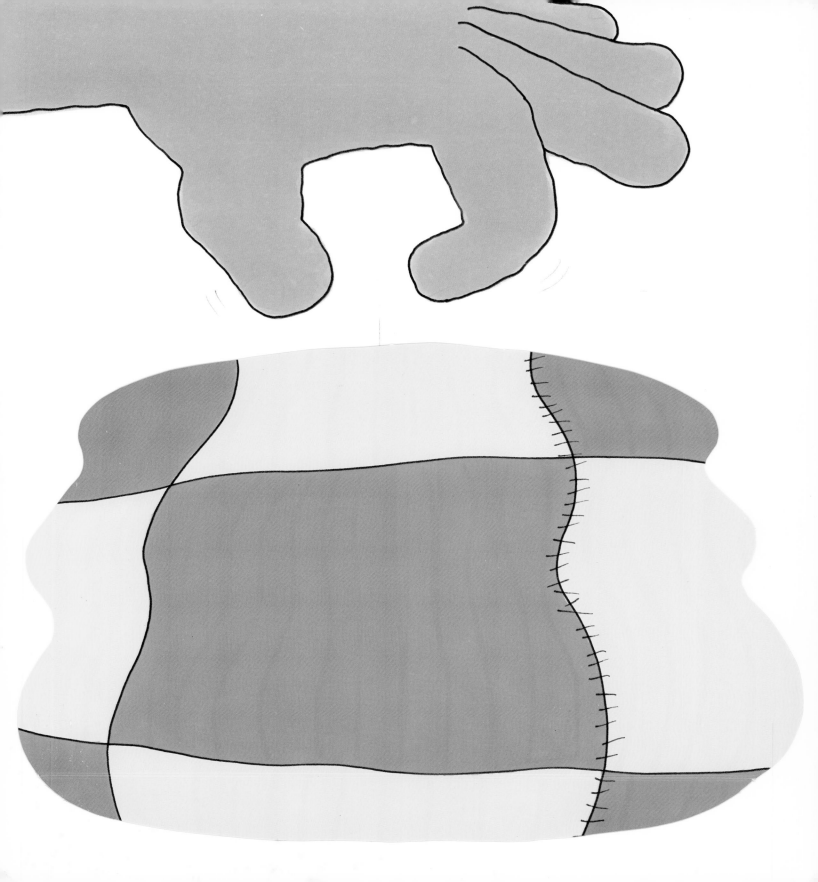

She found a frog.
"Great for a spicy stew!" she said
and flicked Frog into the sack.

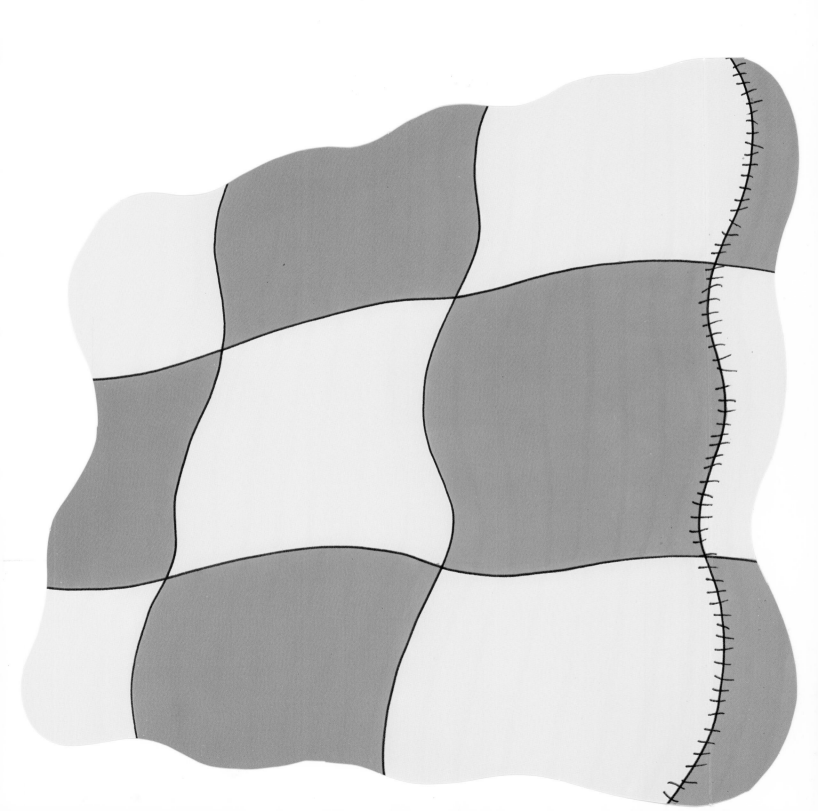

She found a fox.
"Wonderful for a fiery stew!" she
said and pushed Fox into the sack.

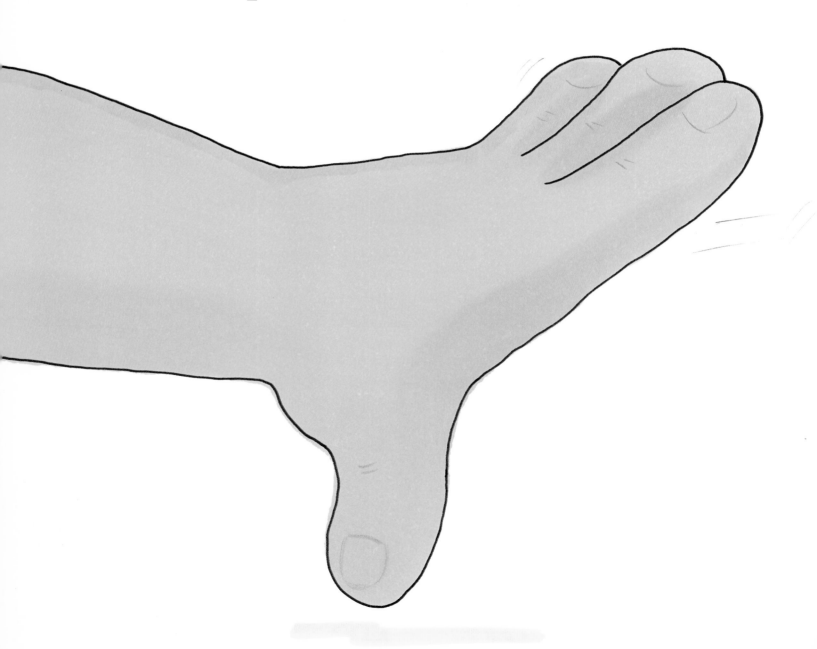

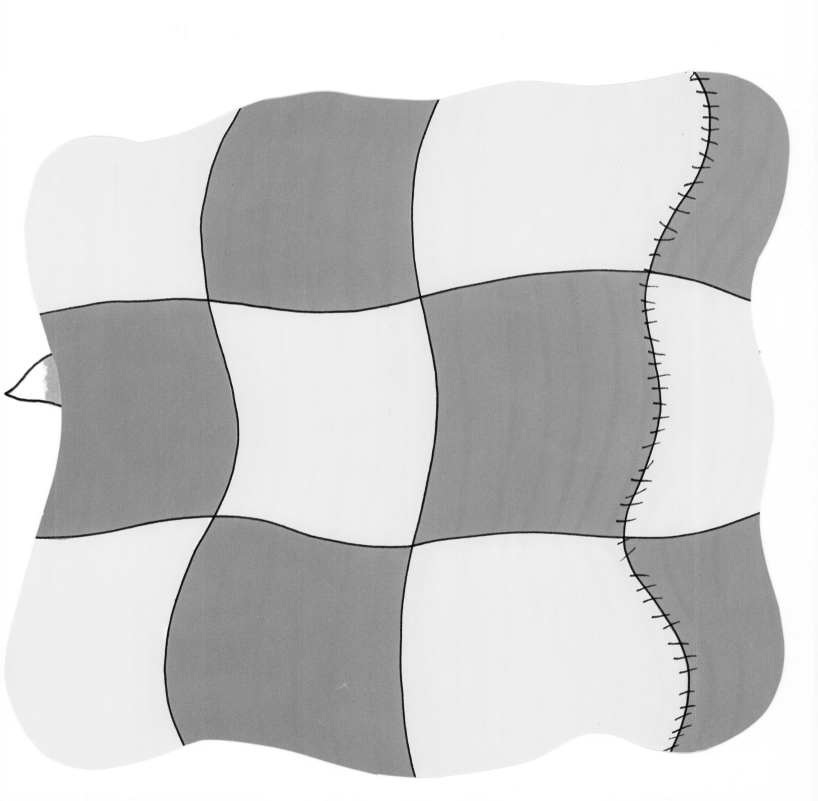

She found a crocodile.
"Marvelous for a snappy stew!"
she said and kicked Crocodile
into the sack.

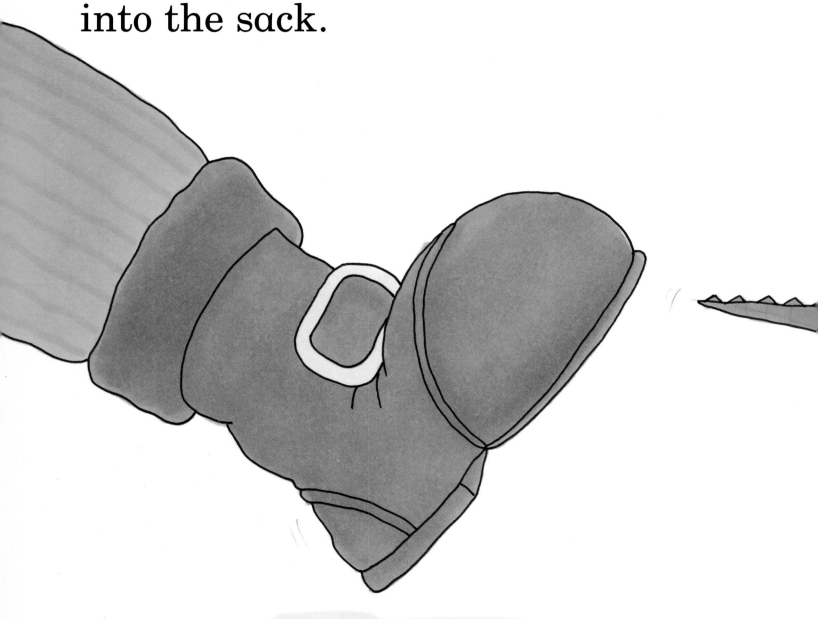

She found a big brown bear.
"Just the thing for a red-blooded
stew!" she said and heaved
Big Brown Bear into
the sack.

Eva the Enormous Giant slung the heavy sack over her shoulder and went into the kitchen. One by one she threw the animals into the enormous cooking pot.
She was very pleased with her morning's catch and sang as she ground the pepper.

While she was grinding, Frog ate
the caterpillar, Fox ate the frog,
Crocodile ate the fox and Big Brown
Bear ate the crocodile.

Big Brown Bear's tummy grew fatter and fatter until he was too fat for the pot. So he climbed out. Big Brown Bear's nose twitched. And twitched. And twitched. There was too much pepper flying around.